The Children of Christmas

Written by Alora Dunlap

Illustrated by Tara Larsen Chang

DEDICATION

For my 3 beautiful children and my 12 wondrous grandchildren
who amaze me every day.
I love you more than there are words.

CONTENTS

Rebecca's Gift   7

James's Treasure   21

Max's Song   33

Simon's Story   43

Hannah's Journey   51

REBECCA'S GIFT

REBECCA'S GIFT

REBECCA was tired. It had been a very long day at the end of a busy week. Since the announcement of the census, people had been pouring into Bethlehem from near and far. Now the city was overflowing; she had never seen so many different people in one place at one time. Wealthy rubbed elbows with poor, shepherds and fishermen with tax collectors. The variety of people drowned the city in noise and activity.

Her father's modest inn had been full several days ago, and yet, this morning he let in another guest. The old woman had been standing outside the inn, hunched over in the cold, cowering against the wall, her gray hair covered in heavy dew. Her father's kind heart allowed him to do the only thing possible, and that was to shift things around again to allow the old woman shelter.

Many of the other innkeepers were taking advantage of the new edict, raising their prices and renting their rooms to those able to pay the price of greed. Rebecca's father was different, not only did he keep his prices the same, but he went a step further and opened his doors to those who were in real need of cover and protection from the elements and crowds of people

7

outside.

Rebecca could not understand why people would want to stay all cooped-up in the packed little inn, the fussing children, the endless debates and conversations of strangers, the smells of cooking and of people who had gone far too long without bathing. It was even beginning to bother her although she had grown up in the inn. She usually loved helping her mother and father. It made her feel so grown-up wearing the big white apron. But this week she looked for any excuse that would take her outside, and when she did escape, she delayed as much as she dared.

As she ran up the stairs again, Rebecca steeled herself. She was taking a blanket to the cooper and his wife. Since they had arrived yesterday they had done nothing but complain. The cooper thought his wealth would buy them a large room and they were angry when all that was left was the small, stuffy storeroom.

She hesitantly knocked on the door and almost fell as the cooper threw it open and yanked the blanket from her. Before the door closed, she heard the sharp voice of the cooper's wife. It seemed her temper had not improved with her nap. The fact that the cooper's wife had a deep cough was the only reason Rebecca's father had even considered renting the room to them. Otherwise he would have turned them away, saving the room for someone who was more civil.

Well, no matter the trouble, the extra money would be nice later in the season when things became slow. Her father had even said that if she would help, and do so cheerfully, she could have a few coins. This would be the first time Rebecca had ever received payment for helping, and she knew what she wanted to do with her first earnings.

SHE had first seen the wool a few weeks ago when she had gone with her mother to Mistress Ruth's to borrow flour. While they visited, she watched as the spinner's swift fingers combed and combed the wool until it glistened in the light. Later, when they returned, the deft fingers spun the newly dyed blue wool. The spindle went around and around pulling the wool and, almost miraculously, creating lengths and lengths of beautiful yarn, yarn so blue that Rebecca got a strange lump in her throat when she looked at it. She had never wanted anything in her young life so badly. Mistress Ruth, seeing the longing in her eyes, gave Rebecca a piece of the blue yarn. Ever since that day, she kept the small treasure tucked safely in the pocket of her skirt where she could touch it and bring it out to look at it over and over again.

Rebecca followed the path of the yarn as it became cloth, and finally ended up at the clothier's shop. Many times, she visited the shop and asked Jonathan to let her touch and hold the cloth. It was as soft as she knew angel wings must be. When her father said she could earn some money, the first thing she did was run to the clothier's and ask him to hold the cloth for her.

Jonathan knew the little girl would never be able to afford the expensive wool.

Jonathan smiled at Rebecca; he liked the little girl, and her visits brightened his day. "This is a lot of wool for a little girl, and it is very expensive; I don't think I can hold it all, but we will see what happens."

A few days later when Rebecca came in, she saw that the blue cloth was gone. Looking up at Jonathan, she knew that he had sold it.

Seeing the disappointment in her eyes, Jonathan said quietly,

"Yes, the cloth was sold, it was very expensive, but . . ."--he then pulled something out from behind his back--"I saved this piece for you, it is small but, I think, big enough to do something with. When you return with your wages, it is yours"

Rebecca's tears of loss became tears of joy. "Oh thank you, I will work really hard, you will see. I'll be back for it."

Jonathan looked sternly at her and then, with a twinkle in his eyes, tucked the cloth out of sight.

JUST this afternoon, Rebecca had snuck back to make sure Jonathan had not sold the cloth. She held it. As always, it felt like holding the sky on a quiet spring day.

As she entered the kitchen, the wonderful aroma of her mother's stew made her stomach grumble. It seemed like it had been an eternity since Rebecca had eaten her dinner. Peeking into the pot, she saw there was a little left in the bottom. She didn't seem needed at the moment, so she scrubbed a bowl and scraped out the last of the stew. Settling herself near the fire, she let out a sigh. Finally, she had a moment to herself. The first bite of stew had just warmed her empty stomach when her mother came in.

"That cooper's wife will drive me mad. The only ones with their own room and they are still not content. I'm sorry Rebecca, but could you take her up some stew?"

"But Mother," exclaimed Rebecca, showing her the bowl, "this is all there is, and I'm starved!"

"Oh, Rebecca," her mother smiled, as she tussled Rebecca's hair, "you are always hungry. I swear you have hollow legs. Take that warm stew up to the cooper's wife, and I will fix you something special. You have been such a help to your father and me. Now run up please and deliver the stew." Her mother placed a piece of bread atop the bowl, gave Rebecca a hug and sent her upstairs.

When the door opened, the bowl was grabbed from her hand, and the slam of the door was all the thanks she received. The rudeness made her wince and it was hard to hold back the tears of anger. Fingering the yarn in her pocket, she thought about the piece of blue cloth. It was what kept her from curling up in a corner somewhere and just sleeping through this night.

As she headed down the stairs, she wished the noise would stop! The constant babble was starting to wear her out, and it was still early. People were arguing and complaining about this new census law. She wished they would start settling down for the evening soon.

The sudden quiet caught her mid-step. She stopped so fast that she almost missed the next stair. Catching herself, she looked around to see what had stilled the guests. People had stopped what they were doing and were looking toward the doorway where her father stood. They seemed, not afraid, but rather awed by what was happening at the door. She moved forward through the people until she stood beside her father. Standing on the other side of the door was a man with his arm around a beautiful young woman. She looked exhausted, as if she couldn't stand another minute. The only thing that kept her from collapsing was the strong arm and shoulder of the man. Still she smiled when she saw Rebecca, and her smile seemed to fill an empty place that the young girl didn't even know existed.

Beside her father, Rebecca heard the man plead, "Please sir, we have traveled so far, and it is my wife's time. She is heavy with child and we have been turned away everywhere. You must have a corner or piece of floor—something."

Rebecca knew the answer right then. There was no room,

not anywhere, and especially not a quiet place to have a baby. She knew something had to be done or the baby was going to be born right here on the step. If Rebecca hadn't already done so, she would have given up her own bed. Looking back into the room, she hoped someone would give up a little space. But the people who had been hushed and reverent just a moment before now nervously looked away and began quiet conversations again. The spell was broken.

Her mother joined them at the door, and upon seeing the young woman, gasped and pulled her into the warm inn and gently sat her down near the hearth.

"Dish up a bowl of that stew," she said. Rebecca ran to the pot and quickly ladled hot stew into a bowl. Hadn't the pot been empty a few minutes ago? Startled, she looked at her mother, but her parents were now in deep conversation.

She set the soup and some bread down in front of the young woman, who once again awarded Rebecca a warm smile. The husband busied himself by fluttering around his wife.

"Joseph," the young woman said gently, "it will be okay, I promise. Here, sit and have a little stew with me. It is going to be a long night." Stopping, he looked into her eyes, smiled sheepishly, and sat down beside her. Putting his arm around her, he looked at her so tenderly that Rebecca had to turn away.

As she stepped away from the young couple, she could hear her mother and father arguing.

"It is all that is left, I just put in new hay. It probably smells fresher than in here, and it will be private."

"But the stable, William? It just doesn't seem right. We should send the cooper and his wife to the stable."

Her father shook his head. "No, the stable will be better than that stuffy room. You will see."

He then took Joseph aside. "All I can offer you is my stable. It is solid, clean and dry. I just put in new hay and I will hobble the animals. I'm sorry I don't have anything else. In fact, I won't even charge you."

Joseph started to object, but the young woman put her hand on his arm. Looking at the innkeeper, she quietly said, "It will be fine, thank you."

Rebecca's father grabbed the lantern from the mantle and led Joseph and his wife to the stable. She began to follow, but her mother stopped her. "Rebecca, go find some blankets, see if the guests can give up any. Bring the extra lantern from the hall, hurry!"

Rebecca was startled by the concerned tone in her mother's voice. Moving quickly, she went from guest to guest asking, and then begging for blankets. Only the family nearest the hearth and the old women that had arrived just this morning were kind enough to offer theirs.

As she retrieved the lantern from the upper landing, the door to the cooper's room opened. The cooper stuck his head out. "Girl, my wife needs another blanket. Give me one of those."

Rebecca clung to her treasures, mustering up all her courage she stuttered, "I'm sorry sir, there is a lady having a baby and the only place for her is in the stable, she needs them more than you."

The cooper turned away. She could hear his wife talking behind the door. Rebecca turned to leave quickly to avoid his wrath, but the cooper called after her, "Girl, wait. Take this blanket too." Turning back, she took the blanket the cooper now held out. Behind him, she could see his wife.

"Let us know what is delivered, will you, child?"

"Yes ma'am, thank you," Rebecca said as she fled. Her arms

were so full, she could barely see.

In the stable, she found everyone in the far corner. Her mother took the blankets from Rebecca and spread them out over the hay, making the young mother as comfortable as possible. Rebecca was surprised at how homey everything looked. Her parents had been busy. Her father had piled up some extra hay and taken the old manger and cut the legs down. It was now a rough cradle awaiting the new baby.

Rebecca knelt beside the improvised cradle and carefully smoothed out the hay. She pulled out twigs and large pieces of straw and smoothed it out again. But it just wasn't soft enough. Looking around worriedly she asked, "Mother, where is the blanket for the baby?"

"Hush, child. Mary has brought some things with her, see?" Rebecca went over to the dark bundle that her mother pointed out. Picking it up she struggled with the knot until it gave way and the contents spilled onto the floor. She carefully laid things aside until she found what she was looking for. Ignoring the hushed voices of the adults, she went back to the manger and spread a small brown blanket over the hay. Sitting back and looking over her handiwork, she frowned. It still didn't look right.

Rebecca was about to protest again when she heard a quiet groan. Turning toward the sound in the corner where the adults were, she heard her mother say, "William, you had better take Rebecca back to the inn and make sure the guests are bedded down and comfortable. Rebecca needs to go to bed soon too."

Rebecca began to object until her mother came over. "Rebecca, can you help mother and start some water on the fire and then find a quiet place and get some sleep? The morning is going to be very busy and I'm going to need your help. I love you very much and you have been such a big girl helping these last couple of weeks. Things will be back to normal soon." With that, her mother brushed Rebecca's hair out of her face, kissed her on the forehead, and gently pushed her toward the inn.

When Rebecca was back inside, she went right to the fireplace and put some water in the big pot over the fire. As she watched the water begin to boil, a frown creased her young face. She was so deep in thought that she didn't hear her father come up beside her. She jumped when she felt his hand on her shoulder. "Little one, you look very tired, it has been a very long day and tomorrow looks like it will be just as busy. You had better go try and get some sleep."

"But Father, I'm worried about the baby. Is everything going to be okay?"

"Yes, Rebecca, now don't fret. Women have babies every day, this is nothing new. Mary may be young but everything will be fine, your mother will see to it. Now get some sleep."

Reluctantly, Rebecca went to her secret place in the back of the inn, curled up, and tried to sleep. But sleep she could not. She kept thinking of the beautiful girl, Mary, and how her smile had filled Rebecca's small soul like a special secret. She remembered how grateful Mary had looked when her father took her and Joseph to the stable; you would have thought it had been a castle. The manger her father had fixed looked comfortable with lots of fresh hay, but what was keeping Rebecca awake was the small, rough, brown blanket.

Things in the inn were quieting down now. Mothers were shushing children, and fathers were finally pulling their families together and curling up in their designated areas for the evening. Others were already fast asleep. Rebecca could hear her father coming and going from the stable, and finally she heard her mother come in.

"I have never seen an easier birth," her mother whispered, "or a mother and child so beautiful!" There is something special about that small family. I couldn't pull myself away."

Rebecca couldn't keep still any longer. Jumping up she ran to her mother and threw her arms around her. "Mother did she have the baby? Did she? What was it? Is everything okay?"

"Yes Rebecca, everything is fine. Mary had a beautiful little boy. He hardly cried at all, just looked around and cooed as if he had something important to say." Hugging her little girl and tipping her chin up, she scolded, "Now why are you still awake?"

With courage born of little sleep and young enthusiasm, Rebecca pulled herself away from her mother and ran to her father. Taking a deep breath, she let the words tumble out. "Father, when people began to arrive you said if I worked hard I could have a few coins. I have tried to be good and help all I can. Have I earned the coins you promised?"

Her father smiled down at her, "Yes, Rebecca, you have. But it is late. We can discuss this in the morning."

Looking up into her father's face, Rebecca pleaded, "Father, I can't wait. Please, it's very important!" and before her father could protest further she pushed ahead. "Can we go to the clothiers? I need to buy something tonight. I'm sure he is still awake with the city so busy. Please? I'll be good for a very long time, I promise."

As anxious tears filled their little girl's eyes, her parents realized the motive behind Rebecca's pleas. Squeezing his wife's hand, the innkeeper hugged his daughter, and wiping her tears away, quietly said, "Yes, Rebecca, we will go right now."

Rebecca could barely keep from running down the street, but her father had a firm grip on her hand. When they arrived at the clothier's, Jonathan was indeed awake as the city was still bustling, even at this time of night. Rebecca pulled her hand from her father's and burst through the door. "Do you still have the blue cloth? Please say that you saved it for me!"

Looking up from his work, Jonathan was surprised to see Rebecca and her father. "Little one, why are you up so late?" he asked, and then giving Rebecca's father a quizzical look, said "William, you didn't have to come down this late with your daughter. I know what a hard worker she is. I saved the cloth for her."

"I know Jonathan, but she has a special purpose for that small piece of cloth and she needs it tonight. Here is the payment, and I'm afraid if you don't get it for her soon, she will wake up the few people who are sleeping tonight with her begging."

Smiling, Jonathan went into the back room, retrieved a small package and handed it to Rebecca. Barely had the money changed hands when she was out the door.

Afraid she would change her mind, Rebecca hesitated for only a moment when she actually held the beautiful cloth as her own. It was so very soft. Daring to rub it against her cheek, she then set her resolve and ran down the street as fast as she could. She didn't stop at the inn, but instead went around back to the stable.

Approaching the stable, she slowed down. The doorway was blocked. Why were all these people here? Did they want to see the new baby, too? Well, it was her stable, and she had an important mission. Pushing through the crowd, she made her way to the corner her father had fixed. Then she came to a sudden stop.

On a cushion of hay sat Mary, now a new mother. Her husband had his arm protectively around his dear wife and the new baby she held. But it was more than this sight that had stopped Rebecca. There was something else about the corner of the stable. For around the small family there was a light, a light not from the lantern, but a light different from any she had ever seen, a light that seemed to hold a secret waiting to be told.

Then Mary looked up and saw Rebecca. As their eyes met, she smiled. The sudden focus of her attention almost made Rebecca forget why she was here. Remembering, she blurted out, "I have a gift for the baby. He needs a soft blanket. Here!" and she all but threw her gift.

Mary looked at the small blue cloth. "Oh, Rebecca, are you sure? It is so beautiful." Unable to speak, Rebecca just nodded. Seeing the conflict in the little girl's eyes, the young mother recognized the value of the gift she had just been given. Softly she asked, "Would you like to help me wrap him in his new blanket?"

Rebecca crept forward, and as she did, the light encircled her, too. She felt like the world had stopped. Again she took the soft blue cloth in her small hands and spread it flat upon the hay. It was the perfect size for a blanket.

Mary then wrapped the baby in the blanket and carefully handed him to Rebecca who didn't hesitate to wrap her arms around the blue bundle.

Rebecca looked down at the baby now in her arms, and he looked back. His eyes were as blue as the cloth, as blue as the sky on a quiet spring day. And she suddenly knew what the light was.

It was love.

REBECCA'S GIFT

JAMES'S TREASURE

JAMES yawned as he sat against the wall with the morning sun warming him. He was feeling very content thanks to a careless farmer who hadn't loaded his donkey securely. The fruit that had fallen to the ground had been an unexpected treat. He felt a little guilty for not alerting the farmer but the gnawing in his stomach had been too intense, so he tried to tell himself it wasn't really stealing if the food fell right at his feet. This rational seemed to quiet some of the guilt of the small boy as he now sat by the gate trying to look as pitiful as he could with the disadvantage of a full stomach. But try as he might he couldn't get the satisfied look off his face.

It was no good; as the sun rose higher in the sky and it began to get hotter, he knew he wouldn't collect much the rest of the day. Too many people were pushing and crowding into the city. A beggar boy was just another obstacle to a final destination: rest after a long journey. So James finally gave in to the comfort of the sun and the fullness of his stomach. He decided to watch and enjoy the parade of people as they flooded through the gates.

Each person that entered the city looked as if he or she had a story to tell. There was the old man hunched over under the weight of his belongings. His face showed that he was someone who had suffered hardship and that this trip had cost him dearly.

Then a rug merchant forced his way through the crowd and trampled anyone in his way as he tried to find a space to set up his rugs. James thought maybe he should have come earlier as space was pretty scarce now.

A large caravan came into the gates with a rich man and his unhappy wife. They looked like they had come a very long way. The dust clung to every inch of them like dew clings to grass. The woman's face was pinched and unhappy and even with her ladies fussing over her, her mood was not improving. Her husband just ignored her pleas, he wasn't happy to be here either.

But it was the families that especially caught James's attention. He watched with an ever-present longing when they came into the city. The father with a child on his shoulder, or a small hand cradled in a large rugged one. The mother brushing the hair out of the face of her son, or carrying a small child in her arms, protecting it from the crowds and the dust. And of course, the brothers and sisters, laughing and teasing, even after an obviously long trip.

JAMES missed his family so very much. Sometimes the longing filled him with such a dark emptiness that he could barely breathe. When the darkness was too much to bear, he would find a place to hide, cry, and wait for the ache to pass.

He still remembered his father coming home and scooping him up in his big, strong arms; it made him feel so safe. His brother, too, had been his protector and friend. Once his brother had proudly said, "This is my brother. He goes where I go."

The memories were happy and painful all at the same time. The yearning, black pain never really went away. It was always just under the surface and gnawed at him continually.

Then sickness invaded their home suddenly, and the whole family became ill. James was strong and recovered quickly. But his father and brother, burdened with work, died in those first dark days.

His mother got well, but it took her a lot longer, and she never regained her full strength. James wondered if it was because of the loss of her husband and son. He wasn't sure but he knew the shadows in her eyes were more than just lingering illness.

At a very young age, James had become the man of the house and he found his hardest task was bringing light back into his mother's eyes. He tried everything. He did extra chores and didn't complain. He picked the small yellow flowers hiding behind the boulders in the field and brought their tender color into their small home. One day he found a kitten cowering behind the butcher's. Together, James and his mother nursed it well. Laughter filled their home as they watched the kitten tumble and play with anything that caught its curious eye. Then one night, it too left them.

His mother did her best to take care of them. She cleaned at a nearby inn. She tried to work at night after James was fast asleep. She would kiss him goodnight and wait until he drifted off before leaving and then return at first light, when he was waking up. The few times she cleaned during the day, she took James with her. His job was to sit in the corner, out of the way, and try to be very quiet. It was hard, but he did his best because he liked visiting the inn. The innkeeper's wife always brought him something to eat, sometimes it was stew or bread and cheese, but he liked the hot meat-filled pastries best. He loved the light crust, but if he bit into it too quickly he would burn his tongue on the bubbling meat and gravy. Sometimes the innkeeper's daughter made faces at him as he ate, but James didn't mind. After all, his stomach was full.

Then his mother got sick again. This time she did not get well.

After that James was on his own. He survived by stealing and begging in the streets. His mother would not have been proud, but sometimes it was hard to think of that when he was cold and hungry.

THESE past few days he hadn't had to beg as much because of all the people in town for the census. All James had to do was keep his eyes open and his wits about him. In the confusion, people were not being very careful and his stomach had been full all week. He knew lean times were just around the corner, but for now he just had to keep out of sight of the centurions, and that was fairly easy because they were so busy keeping the peace and shuffling people around.

The sun was going down and James was getting cold. He knew he would have to find a safe place to sleep soon. Only a few people were straggling in now, but one couple caught his attention.

The man carried a heavy load on his back and his wife rode

a donkey. She was beautiful! That was what James had first
noticed. But it was the way she had her arms wrapped around
her that piqued his curiosity. Her husband would steady her on
the donkey but she wouldn't let go of what she clutched to her.
James followed them through the city trying to get a glimpse of
the mysterious object she held that seemed so precious. As
they went from one inn to another, he overheard the man
asking for a room. James shook his head, he knew the man
would not be able to find shelter anywhere; the city was full.

He followed them to the inn owned by William. James knew
there wasn't any room here. As he listened from the shadows,
his knowledge was confirmed. Meanwhile the innkeeper's wife
came to the door and said something to her husband. After a
short discussion, they all disappeared into the inn. Well, maybe
they did indeed have a corner for the couple. He remembered
the innkeeper's wife was a very kind person and he thought at
least the couple would have something good to eat.

His entertainment gone, James slipped into the stable
behind the inn. He had made a habit of checking this particular
place every day and often slept here. This was the same inn his
mother used to clean so long ago, and in a strange way, it made
him feel safe.

The other great thing about this stable was that the
innkeeper had become absentminded in his old age and often
James would find the remnants of a meal left behind in haste
or forgetfulness. James had been able to eat often because of
this carelessness. At the very least, it was a warm and safe place
to spend the night.

James made his way to the back of the stable. Suddenly,
there was William in the stable. James scurried out a window as
the innkeeper began to put more hay on the ground. What was

he up to? James wondered. Then William brought the cow and goats out into the yard and hobbled them to the side of the inn. This was strange behavior, but James was tired, so he snuggled up between two goats that had settled for the night. The animals' breathing soothed him like a lullaby. As he slept the sound sleep of a child, James didn't hear the comings and goings of the innkeeper and the young couple. But ultimately the disturbances grew loud enough to break through his slumber and he was jolted awake.

Rubbing his eyes, he peeked through the window and pulled back in fear. The stable was full of people! His first reaction was to leave quickly but curiosity soon overtook his fear. Carefully, he climbed back through the window and tried to peer around animals and people. From the look of awe on their faces he could see something important was in the stable! Wiggling around some more he could see that the man and women he had followed to the inn were here, and that they seemed to be the reason for all the fuss.

Suddenly James remembered how the woman was holding something very close to her when she was on the donkey. Maybe they had brought a great treasure with them.

James could tell the treasure was in the manger, but no matter how hard he tried, he couldn't see what it was. Frustrated, he scooted back to the far corner of the stable. Well, these people couldn't stay here forever. He would just wait.

The idea of having a priceless treasure filled James's young mind. He kept himself occupied by thinking of all the comforts that he would buy himself: a warm bed with a big blanket, a meal that he could eat sitting down at a table, not on the run or crouched, hiding in some corner. Oh, and a new pair of sandals! His had worn his out long ago and the bottoms of his feet were now almost as tough as leather.

Well, this treasure was as good as his. All he had to do was be patient and careful. He had to get to it before others did.

As his mind wandered, he began to think of his mother. James tried not to remember her, because he was ashamed of how he stole to survive. His mother had been an honest and hardworking woman, but still, they didn't have much and when she got sick again, there had been no extra money for food, let alone medicine or a doctor. That was when James began to steal. He had tried to find work, but he was always told he was too young. The shopkeepers just laughed and shooed him away. So he used his smallness to his advantage and found food enough for the two of them. Whenever his mother asked, he would lie and say it was the kindness of neighbors. But he had been afraid of the neighbors. He had heard from the other street boys about the slavers and he was afraid he would be taken away and sold. And who would take care of his mother then? he thought. At the end, he lay by her body, and as it became cold, so did his small heart. Finally, only looking back once, he left her in that little room.

The quietness suddenly pulled him out of his sad thoughts. How long had he been letting his mind wander? Shaking the memories away, he carefully moved close again. Everyone was gone now except for the man and woman. They lay together, asleep in the corner. The manger with its treasure was right in front of them. James crept forward very slowly. He struggled to move silently. His heart was beating so hard that he was sure it could be heard. He didn't know when someone might come in or how deeply the couple slept. As he moved, the hay rustled beneath him and sounded loud in his ears. Cautiously, he continued his journey, stopping every few seconds to make sure the man and women did not stir. It seemed to take such a long time, but now the manger was between him and the couple. He was almost there.

All of a sudden, he began to worry about the size of the treasure. If it were large, would it be too heavy for him? If it were a bag of coins would they make a lot of noise? Why hadn't he thought of these things before? Now it was too late, he couldn't turn back.

When he finally made it to the manger, he tried to peer between the cracks to see exactly what was inside. He could see nothing. Very carefully, he reached up the side of the rough wood and began to feel around. Hay, now cloth, very fine cloth. This must indeed be a great treasure to be carried in such soft, expensive, material. Then, as his hand moved slowly along the inside of the manger, his finger was unexpectedly encircled! It took James only a split second to realize the small hand of a baby had caught him!

James was filled with all kinds of emotions. He felt stupid, then disappointed, and then afraid! And what was worse, he couldn't pull his hand away because if he did he might awaken the baby. Somehow he had to extract himself from the strong grip. Cautiously he looked over the top of the manger and came face to face with two bright eyes; these eyes did not have the blank unaware look of most babies. The eyes that were looking back at him were full of love and understanding.

In that moment James felt the steel bands around his heart burst. For the love that was coming from this baby was the same love that he had felt in his mother's arms. Without warning, the pain he had buried so deep surged out of him and he began to sob. Tears flowed down his cheeks and fell onto the blanket. The baby continued to hold tightly onto his finger and look at him with those beautiful eyes.

When James felt like he had been completely drained of sorrow and pain, and he could cry no longer, he abruptly remembered where he was. Looking up he saw the couple was awake; they smiled and looked at him tenderly. Then he felt arms around his small shoulders, his first instinct was to flee! But he was so exhausted from crying that he just could not make himself move or pull his hand away from that tiny one.

Resigning himself to his fate, he looked to see who his captor was. It was the old innkeeper holding him. He knew he was in trouble, and he would go to jail or worse. But for some reason, the fear would not stick. Then he realized the innkeeper was calling him by name.

"James, there you are! We have been looking for you everywhere. We left food for you, hoping you would remember our inn. We promised your mother we would care for you, but by the time we knew she was gone, you had disappeared."

It took the innkeeper saying it several times over before the words sank in. James finally realized, for the first time in months, that he was safe. Someone wanted to take care of him.

Looking down at the baby, James took a deep breath and the empty hollowness that he had carried for so long was gone. James felt like he was bursting and that the love that filled him was so big that even his skin glowed with joy. James now knew that the small baby was indeed a great treasure. That this baby was not an ordinary baby in an ordinary manger.

With a small sigh, the baby let go of James's finger and began to fuss. Suddenly, the everyday cries of a hungry baby and the comforting murmurs of a mother broke the magic of the moment. James smiled; he knew the love he had felt during

those few minutes would
stay with him forever.

He turned and
instinctively hugged the
innkeeper, who wrapped his
arms around the little boy.
James now knew he had
found a home.

JAMES'S TREASURE

MAX'S SONG

WHAT a glorious day! Even the clouds looked as if they were rejoicing as they did somersaults through the sky, jostling each other to be first in some imaginary race. The time for the Advent was so near, and it seemed as if the very air would burst with excitement and shout with delight. The streets of Heaven had not been this busy since The Creation. Everyone seemed to have some place to be and something to do. Nothing was standing still.

Humming, Max skipped to rehearsal, his wings fluttering behind him like a cape. He felt like he was smiling all over and it even seemed to be tickling his insides. He almost laughed out loud as the joy tried to tumble out. He filled his lungs with the crisp morning air and opened his mouth to let the song escape. He couldn't help it. He always had a melody tripping about in his mind, knocking up against his thoughts, and clamoring for attention.

Max heard music everywhere. It wrapped itself about him and made him feel whole. He heard it in the everyday things, the water swirling around rocks, the leaves whispering in the

33

wind, even the sound of footsteps on the street soon left him with a melody jumbling in his head. He sometimes felt as if he were made of music and that when he sang, his thoughts grew wings and took flight on the air around him like a beautiful bird.

WHEN Max first heard about the auditions for The Announcement he was one of the first in line to try out. He had been so excited, and then, he had not been chosen. Max was crushed.

The choir director had told him that his voice was one of the purest he had heard and that Max's passion for the music had surprised him, but that he needed to work on his "technique."

The director said, "When singing with a choir many voices needed to sound like one."

Max was confused and disappointed. He didn't even know what technique meant. The director had suggested he go see Brother Arnold and had kindly said that maybe there would be time to try again if Max worked very hard. He walked away dejected but willing to try.

Brother Arnold was kind and worked many hours with him. Max didn't know that singing could be so complicated, but he worked hard and finally Brother Arnold felt Max was ready to try again. When he found out the audition would be in front of the whole choir, Max almost didn't set up the appointment. But this was important to him and the music wouldn't let him give up. He had to try, even if it was only for a fill-in part.

On the day of the audition, Max was terrified, but he gathered up his courage, cleared his throat, and shook away his doubts. Closing his eyes, he focused on the song. Then he took a deep breath and showed the music how to go. That was the trick he had learned from Brother Arnold, how to control the music and help it to find its way.

When he was done, complete silence greeted him. He opened his eyes, but couldn't look up. He must have failed again. Dejectedly he turned to leave. Suddenly he felt an arm around his shoulder. Max looked up at the choir director through tears of frustration.

"Don't go Max," the choir director smiled down at him, "there is a place for you in the choir now. I never imagined so much beauty could come from one so small."

And then the whole choir cheered and welcomed him. He was a member of The Announcement Choir! It was almost too much to believe. If there really were such a thing as a Cloud Nine, he would be on it. Smiling from ear to ear and feeling as if his face would break, he took his place with the others.

They had been practicing for what seemed like forever and had gone through several directors. It seemed like every time things started to click, the choir director would be sent down to do his turn on Earth. Max had weathered out the annoyed looks of each new director and had proven that even though he was small, he was worthy, and indeed a key element of The Choir. The new director, Sister Judith, had even given him a special part.

WITH a start, Max pulled himself out of his memories and realized he was going to be late. Breathless, he finally reached the choir room. He quickly pulled his robe over his head, squirming until it hung right. Brushing out a wrinkle, he scooted into the room and slid into his spot between Cynthia and Emily. Whew! Being small sometimes had its advantages.

Emily turned and poked him. "I thought maybe you decided to drop out."

He looked up and saw her grinning at him.

Cynthia was quietly laughing, too. "Good thing Sister Judith is distracted today."

Max grinned back, if he didn't like Cynthia and Emily so much he would have resented being placed with the girls. But the three of them had become close friends. Many times after choir they would find a quiet place and watch the happenings on Earth. It was always fascinating to see how people handled life. The trio would cheer on and celebrate when they saw accomplishments, and cry when they saw sorrow or disappointment. But mostly they would sit around and imagine what their turn on Earth would be like.

Nervously, Max tried to brush out the invisible wrinkles again. Looking around he noticed he wasn't the only one who was a little tense. The whole choir was fidgeting and there seemed to be more than the normal amount of throat clearing. Sister Judith looked the most nervous of all, for this was the day that Father was coming to listen to the arrangement for the first time.

When she had first taken over The Choir, Sister Judith had listened to the arrangement and then sent the singers away. When they met again there was new music. And what music it was! It almost leapt from the page. It was so exciting and joyful that they learned it quickly. The notes and their voices expressed the message even without the words.

But today Sister Judith didn't look quite as confident of her stray from tradition. Father had come in to give encouragement. The Choir watched Sister Judith and began on cue. As they worked their way through the music, Max knew things were not going well. Finally the last note rang out. It had been good, but everyone knew they could have done better.

Father smiled and said it was beautiful. He was pleased that the music was joyous and thanked The Choir for all their hard work. But after he left and the excitement died down, everyone knew they had work ahead of them. They had missed a couple of marks and everyone had seemed a note behind. Sister Judith was distressed, and they were all sent home to practice, practice, practice.

And practice Max did. He sang when he did his chores and as he ran errands. He climbed the mountaintops and sang out his part to the clouds. He went to the caverns so he could hear his voice as it rang against the walls. He sang scales and warbled at the birds and practiced holding the notes as long as he could. He worked on all the things Brother Arnold had taught him. Max even hummed in his sleep.

The day of the last rehearsal arrived and Max felt like he had a flock of butterflies in his stomach. How was he going to sing with all this fluttering going on? Controlling the urge to shout his nervousness away, Max hummed to himself all the way to the hall. Father was there again! Max was surprised, Father had so much to do, but He said He wanted to hear the choir one more time.

Father visited the choir whenever He could. Last time He had spoken to them he told them that the message of the angels would be remembered forever and would fill the hearts of men with gladness and peace long after the last note had disappeared into the night. It made Max's heart swell to think of how he was part of such an important event.

Max took his place and attempted to still the butterflies. The choir began to sing. As the music filled the air, it took on a life of its own and wove its message about them, filling the air with light. Max was so caught up with the beauty they were creating that suddenly he realized it was time for his solo, his one line. It was so very important. He closed his eyes, breathed in, opened his mouth and then—nothing. Not even a squeak! The music hung in the air for a brief moment before it faded like gossamer.

The room became hushed and then quiet whispering replaced the silence. Cynthia and Emily stared at him in disbelief. Sister Judith approached him. "Max, are you okay?"

Max swallowed, looked up, and tried to speak. He fought back a feeling of panic as he turned to his friends. He tried to talk, but again, nothing.

"Oh Max," Cynthia cried as she tried to hug him, but Max shrugged her away. He could not endure the looks of sympathy and concern, and the thought of Father's disappointment made his heart sink. Unable even to apologize, he ran from the room, and kept running until his tears stopped him and the sobs of disappointment shook his small shoulders.

As the day progressed, Max's voice slowly returned, but all he could do was hum or sing very, very softly. He would not be able to rejoin the choir. Brother Arnold, Emily, and Cynthia had stopped by to see how he was doing, but when they left they looked as unhappy as he felt. Even Sister Judith came to check on him. It was all he could do to be brave when she said it was okay and that Jeffrey was going to fill in for him.

"It won't be the same," she said, trying to comfort him. But he did not feel very comfortable. He felt sad and his heart hurt.

Max left his room as the time neared. He went to a spot

where he could look down on Earth. Even in his misery he couldn't miss The Advent.

It was a moment that filled him with so much gratitude. His big brother had gone to Earth for him. He watched as The Choir descended to deliver the message and felt another twinge of disappointment. But soon the beauty of the music and its message replaced the sorrow in his heart with joy.

He met The Choir as they returned and when he found Emily and Cynthia, they hugged each other and started talking all at once. The girls told and retold their part of the story, and in his quiet voice, Max told them the other part, the part that he had seen from above. As they quietly listened, tears ran down their faces. Love, Music, and Joy had filled the evening on Earth and in Heaven.

They had been sharing and retelling the story well into the evening when Brother Arnold approached them. "Max, I have a request from Father." Stunned, Max listened as Brother Arnold relayed the Father's message. Cynthia and Emily's faces showed the same surprise and astonishment that he felt. Brother Arnold continued. "We only have a moment; do you accept his request?"

Numbly, Max nodded and answered in a hushed "Yes."

As they descended into the heavy air, and through the twinkling of dawn, Max could see The Star, the one that would guide others, and then he saw the lights of Bethlehem. Silently they made their way through the city. Gently they moved around sleeping people, people unaware of the miracle happening this night. They quietly passed guards and animals that were just beginning to stir as night began to slowly slip away.

They reached the small inn and then the even smaller stable.

Brother Arnold stopped at the stable door. "I will wait here. This is your mission. Now go and serve well."

Max crept into the stable. He found the family at the back of the last stall. They had dropped off in an exhausted sleep and Joseph had his arm protectively around Mary. Father had given them the strength to get through the day and long night, but now weariness had taken over.

Looking around, he saw the simple manger. Could mortals see the love that glowed from the rough box? Reverently he looked down at the baby. This was The Christ, Jesus, his brother. The lump in his throat almost stopped him right there. He loved his brother so very much.

He had not been able to shout in glorious announcement of His birth, but this mission gave him even more joy. The baby was beginning to stir. Looking over at Mary and Joseph, he knew he had been given a very important responsibility. They had many heavy days ahead of them. Rest and comfort would become a luxury.

Again the baby stirred and began to fuss. Max wondered what could make his brother want to cry. Did all that skin itch? Well, he would know soon enough when it was his turn on Earth, but now he had a mission to complete. He felt so blessed to be given this small part in the very large plan. Looking up he quietly whispered, "Thank you, Father."

He looked down, knelt beside the crude bed and began

to hum. Then, very quietly, he voiced his love and gratitude to the very wee babe, his brother, who would sacrifice all and suffer greatly for him. As he softly sang his lullaby, the baby quieted and drifted back to sleep.

SIMON'S STORY

THE night sky exploded with light and music. The shepherds, frozen with delight and fear, listened in amazement. Angels were singing of a marvelous gift given to them this day, "Glory to God in the highest, and on earth, peace and goodwill to all."

Simon stood with the others staring with wonder and awe into the heavens. What did it mean? They were saying the Savior was here! He was born! And that they, lowly shepherds, were to witness this blessed event.

The sky was quiet now and the shepherds were getting ready to go. Simon would be the one to stay with the sheep. Why him? Just because he was the youngest? He wanted to go, to follow the star and see this miracle that the angels had described, but someone had to stay with the sheep. So Simon stood watching as the others made their way into Bethlehem.

Why would a Savior come as a baby? Shouldn't He come and fill the sky with lights and glories Himself? How could a baby save the Jews and deliver them from the Great Roman Empire? Simon did not understand the complexity of it all. He was just a small shepherd boy who sat on a hill, day and night, tending the sheep as they grazed.

Simon didn't want to be a shepherd, but his father was a shepherd, and his grandfather had been a shepherd. It seemed as if everyone in his family was a shepherd, everyone, that is, except Mathias. Uncle Mathias was a fisherman. Once, Simon had visited his uncle in Tiberius. He had seen the fishing boats, smelled the water and had even helped pull in the nets full of fish. The day he stood on that boat he knew that was where he belonged.

But tonight here he was in a field, watching sheep, alone. Why did he feel so glum? After all, he had just witnessed an amazing sight. Angels had filled the sky with music and light. Yes, the Savior must be here! How he wished he could have gone to Bethlehem.

The sun was high in the sky when the men finally returned. All night Simon had been with the sheep while they had made the journey into Bethlehem. As they approached he could hear them talking.

"He was beautiful, and the mother, so fair!"

"Our Savior, born in a stable!"

On and on they spoke of the things they had seen. But the small boy, exhausted from watching the sheep during the long dark night, did not care. Simon was tired and cross. Handing over the crook to his older brother, he stomped home to crawl into bed.

When Simon woke up, late in the day, he could hear the buzz of excited conversation. Several people were in his house, and they were all talking about the miracles they had seen.

Simon spoke up, "I saw the angels." Everyone looked toward him.

His little sister, Sarah, asked, "Did you see the baby?"

He hung his head. "No I stayed and watched the sheep."

"Oh," the others said, and turned back to the shepherds

who had gone into Bethlehem. Simon was hurt that they had so quickly disregarded him. His mother came up behind him.

"Simon, that was a fine thing you did, staying with the sheep. I am so proud of you"

"Yes mother," he mumbled, and he went to get ready to go back to the fields.

Over the next few days, his home was filled with people who wanted to talk to his father and brothers about what they had seen, so Simon spent many days in the fields with the sheep. The whole idea of a Savior was beginning to feel pretty far-fetched to him. Some Savior. Since His coming, He hadn't saved Simon from anything. In fact, now Simon had even more responsibilities, and had to work even harder. Feelings of anger slowly replaced his memory of the angels, until soon he wasn't sure if he had really seen them at all.

Finally, his mother took pity on him. She told his father that she needed Simon to go into Bethlehem to pick up some things for her. Grudgingly, his father agreed, and now he was free, at least for the day. All thoughts of angels, babies, and sheep quickly fled his mind as it filled with thoughts of a new adventure.

Simon practically ran the whole way, only slowing down when he reached the gates of Bethlehem. He stopped inside the walls to catch his breath. The smells from the vendor stalls and the noise of the crowds were almost overwhelming, but Simon found it exciting after the quiet of the hills. The city was so full it seemed as if the walls would burst.

For weeks people had been arriving from all over the country for the census. Now that the counting was done, everyone was in a hurry to leave for home. Shopkeepers yelled from doorways and stalls, trying to get as much business as they could from people looking for last minute supplies.

Simon walked along, enjoying the bustle of the city. There was so much to see that he didn't pay attention to where he was going, and bumped into a man carrying several small packages.

"Oh, I'm sorry!" He exclaimed as he looked up.

"That's alright," said the man as he steadied Simon. "The streets are very busy today, and I'm not really watching where I am going, either."

As they turned to go their separate ways, the man stopped and called to Simon, "Do you know of a cobbler here in Bethlehem?"

Simon looked again at the stranger. Kindness showed through his tired eyes, "Yes, I'll take you to Timothy. Follow me."

Simon led the way through the streets until they came to the door of the cobbler shop. "It isn't as fancy as some," Simon apologized, "but Timothy will give you a fair price."

"Thank you," said the man, as he dropped a coin into Simon's hand.

Simon smiled, he felt great for having done a good deed, and getting rewarded for it too!

He went back to the main part of town and picked up the items his mother had sent him for. With his newfound wealth, he purchased a pomegranate. He decided that one half he would eat on the way back and the other half he would save for his mother. It would be a wonderful surprise for her. His mouth watered with anticipation, but he wanted to wait until he ate his lunch. There was a big old tree outside the gates that would be a perfect place for him to stop before he continued home.

With his stomach anticipating the promise of food, he left the city. As he approached the tree, he noticed that someone else was already there. He was a little disappointed that the shade wouldn't be all his, but he decided that there was room enough for two. Simon walked to the far edge of the shade of the great tree and sat down to eat.

It had been a long day, and he was famished. As he ate, he stole a quick glance at his companion. She was humming and talking to the baby she held in her arms. He could hear her say, "He'll be back in a little bit, shh, he went for a few supplies for our trip. Sleep, Little One, so mother can rest before we start for home."

But the baby was having none of it. Simon sympathized; he had a baby sister. Whenever she started really fussing, his mother would get frustrated and then it seemed like nothing could calm the child. At times like this, Simon would often take his sister out so his mother could rest. The change of scenery was enough of a distraction that the fretting would soon stop.

Just then the mother looked over at Simon. "He's a bit upset at me. I don't think this traveling agrees with him," she said with a smile.

Simon was surprised at the tiredness in her voice. Awkwardly, he said, "Maybe I could hold him for a while. I'll be very careful; I help my mother with my baby sister all the time."

The young mother seemed to hesitate for a moment and then said, "Thank you, maybe I could rest for just a moment."

As Simon reached for the baby, he remembered the uneaten pomegranate in his hand. He set the prized fruit beside her as he took the baby. Once again she looked up at him and smiled.

Simon took the small bundle and began to walk around in the shade of the tree. He hummed quietly, for he didn't want anyone to hear. Finally the baby quieted. Gently he pulled the blanket back and as the cover fell away, two bright blue eyes looked up at him. Simon was startled. The baby had been so quiet that he was sure he had been asleep. He turned back to the mother, but she had fallen asleep against the tree. "Well," he said, "I guess we're on our own."

Simon went back to his coat and sat down, carefully putting the baby on his lap. The baby stared at him with what seemed to be curiosity, so Simon began to talk to him. He told him about his home and family—about the sheep and the angels that had come to the field. Then he began talking of his dream to someday fish with his uncle. On and on he went, telling his stories and bearing his small heart to this wee babe, who watched him all the while with what seemed to be great intent.

"You are a kind boy. Your mother must be proud of you."

The voice startled Simon and he looked up quickly. It was the man he had led to the cobbler's shop, and beside him stood the baby's mother. How long had they been there? Had they heard him telling the baby his secrets?

The man went on. "First you help me, and then you come back and help my wife. I don't know how to thank you."

Simon stood up and started to hand the baby back to his mother. Tenderly she looked at Simon and said, "His name is Jesus."

The memories of that night in the field, the sky filled with light and the angels' message, "You shall find the babe wrapped in swaddling clothes lying in a manger and his name shall be Jesus."

Simon looked again at those two bright blue eyes. Wonder and amazement filled him with joy. Yes, he knew it was true! This small helpless baby was the Savior! Suddenly he wasn't ready to give Him back. He needed to hold Him longer, feel His love. He had so much to tell Him, but the parents were waiting. The mother held out her arms to take the precious child back.

The small boy pulled the baby close to him, kissed his warm cheek and then whispered in his ear. "I will watch for you. Remember me. My friends call me Peter."

HANNAH'S JOURNEY

HANNAH was hiding again. She knew she would be missed soon and have to go back to the garden.

She had found this hiding place not long after she was brought to the palace. She had been carrying a small meal to the princesses when she tripped, scattering the food on the ground. She had been immediately punished for her clumsiness. As she crawled on the ground picking up the mess, she noticed a wall stuck out and didn't meet the other. There was a sliver of a shadow showing a small opening. Her curiosity nagged at her and she snuck back later to investigate. Looking around, making sure no one was watching, she stepped between the walls. The space wasn't very big, she squeezed along the opening until she came to the edge and found herself behind a heavy drape, and then she heard the King below. With a start she froze. Then realized she was behind the curtain that hung at the back of the King's throne. She forced herself against the wall and tried to melt into it. She would be in so much trouble if she was discovered. The King yelled again and stormed out of the room with everyone following behind like children playing follow the leader. The doors slammed shut with a heavy thud. Breathing out heavily Hannah realized she had been holding her breath. Slowly her panic was being replaced with curiosity and she tried to find a way to look through the curtain. There was a small gap where two of the curtains met and she peered through and gasped again. The room was beautiful! Ceiling, walls and floor were white marble that glistened in the light. Everything was gilded with gold and jewels and red carpets and drapes hung about heavy and rich. She wanted to stay longer and fill herself with its splendor but didn't know how long she had been gone and didn't want to be punished again for being absent. Carefully she retreated and was able to escape they eyes of any adults. She hurried back to the garden. No one had even noticed she had been gone.

Hannah's official title was Royal Playmate, but some days she felt more like an old rag doll. The princesses only played with her when they were bored and by then they were usually grumpy and mean. Of course she would not complain. She had done that once and found out quickly that the princesses could do no wrong.

So whenever Hannah could, she snuck into the secret place. There she could watch the comings and goings of the court and escape into fantasies about the people from other lands who visited the King. Some had hair that glittered like gold and there were men whose faces were so covered by hair they seemed like giant bears. The ones from the orient were so graceful it seemed like they slid across the floor as if by magic. And they always brought the most wonderful gifts; musical instruments, fruits and vegetables. And of course there was always gold and precious gems that poured out of trunks and boxes like rivers. But Hannah liked the animals best, except the snakes. And one time she had almost been discovered by a curious monkey!

Today she sat in her secret place, a little bored. It was early enough; maybe the princesses would still be in a good mood. She could entertain them with the new puppets they had just received from China. After all, Hannah was very good at pretend. She was just starting to slowly move away, when three men came in and caught her attention.

The way they carried themselves made Hannah stop. It wasn't the fine clothes they wore or their regal bearing; there was something else about them. She wasn't sure what it was, but she was curious and strained to listen.

They introduced themselves as Caspar, Melchior and Balthasar, learned men from the East, Magi who studied prophecies and historical events. They said they had brought gifts for the New King. Herod gave a start and Hannah heard his voice become tense and silky. Hannah knew this was bad, and she shivered.

"New king? What new king?" Herod asked in a curious tone.

Caspar bowed low, "Your Majesty, we have studied the prophecies and legends for many years and when the new star appeared we knew it was time for the birth of the New King, the one who would be King of the Jews. We traveled far to come here to the palace to see him."

The King tried to hide the anger that was building in him, "There is no New King here, but stay, refresh yourselves. I will counsel with my advisors and see if we can help you find this King."

The three visitors did not notice people slowly moving out of the room. The courtiers had recognized the look in the King's eyes and his honeyed voice, and did not want to be near him when the Magi left. The room was so tense Hannah didn't want to even breathe; she stepped back as far away from the curtains as she could.

When the Magi left, the King curtly dismissed anyone who was lingering. There were several minutes of hurried footsteps and quiet whispers as visitors and courtiers quickly left the throne room. With everyone moving about Hannah was too frightened to move, then it was too quiet for her to slip away.

Only the King and his advisors remained, and Hannah, cowering behind the curtain, hoped she would not be discovered. Very slowly, and in a deadly quiet voice, the King asked, "What do you know of this prophecy of a King of the Jews?"

The advisors stuttered, murmured, and looked away. Finally, one spoke out. "Your Majesty, there is such a prophecy, but we didn't pay it much heed. King of the Jews? That would be you, mighty King Herod, who is King over all the lands."

The King responded in a very low voice. "I want to know more, bring me the information you have on this prophecy. If it brought learned men from the east here, then I want to know what it says."

The advisors left quickly; The King exploded in anger; he picked up the nearest vase and threw it after the scurrying advisors and then shouting, raged out of the room. In the deafening silence Hannah crept out and went to the garden to shake off the unease she felt. There she ran right into one of the princesses who looked her up and down and only said, "Are you still here?"

AS Hannah sat in her room waiting to be summoned again, she

thought about her life before she had been brought to the castle. She missed her family so much. She had loved playing with her sister and helping her mother with her baby brother. When her father came through the door he would hug her and ask, "How is my little dreamer today?" And she missed family prayers and the stories her father told. She felt so alone here.

Hannah remembered, with a shudder, the day a man from the castle and his entourage had stopped in front of their door. She had been sitting quietly by the well and watched him approach with curiosity. When he went into the house, she listened at the window and heard the angry discussion between the stranger and her father. The next thing she knew, she was clutching a small bundle of her belongings and weeping as she frantically tried to hold on to her mother.

Gently, her father pulled her away. He wrapped his arms around her then took her face in his hands. "Hannah, this must be. I can't explain to you why, but I know all will be well. Be brave." He had then put a small coin in her hand. "Hannah keep this deep in your pocket, when you touch it remember your family and your God." She remembered the sad look in his eyes, and then she was hoisted into the cart.

Tears filled her eyes as Hannah remembered this last scene. She wanted to go home. She wondered if she would be sent away soon, since the princesses had new playmates from distant lands and were becoming more and more tired of her.

UNBELIEVABLY, the next morning Hannah was dismissed from the castle by the nanny, Ursula. She was told that she would leave in the afternoon. Hannah forgot everything else and flew to her cot below the kitchen to gather up her few things.

As she paced back and forth awaiting instruction, she remembered that the Magi were going to see the King today and ask if he had further instructions for them. Their presence had been so powerful, and their story so mysterious that Hannah wanted to find out what was going to happen. She had time, so quietly she made her way to her secret place.

Hannah got there just in time. The learned men were before the King. Herod seemed very calm. "I have listened to my councilors, they have found many legends and stories, but they say they are all just hearsay and stories mothers tell to their children. There is no truth in them. You have come such a long way, stay and enjoy the many comforts I can offer before you return home."

Caspar, the oldest of the men, stepped forward and explained that this was not merely a tale or story that had been passed down, but a prophecy of a great birth. He then explained the prophecies told of many things that would come to pass because of the birth of this great King. The words of the ancients had said, "He shall be King over all, and every knee will bow down to him."

Hannah could see Herod's hand tighten on the arm of the throne. "Very well, continue your journey," he said. Disguising his anger and steadying his voice, "Please return to me with the location of this New King that I might also bring him great gifts and worship him."

With that the three men left, and Hannah heard the king whisper to his head advisor, "When they return we will go, indeed; but we will go and kill this so-called child king. No one will be greater than I."

As soon as she could, Hannah quietly and carefully left. She knew she must warn the men from the east, these Magi. She wondered how she could get to them in time. She knew her way around the palace but outside of its protective walls she would be lost. Maybe if she hurried she could catch them at the gate, but as she rushed out she was intercepted by Ursula. "Hannah, it's time for you to go. You will ride with the wine merchant, Abar. He is traveling in the same direction as your home."

Hannah's heart jumped, maybe now she could catch up with the Magi even if they were outside the city walls. She ran and got her things and then dashed to the stables. But Abar wasn't quite ready to leave. Hannah tried to be patient, but her heart was pounding. She knew they had to leave soon or there would be no chance to catch the Magi.

Finally Abar was ready to go and Hannah climbed up on the wagon beside him. Abars' mules seemed to be as old as he was, and they started slowly on their journey.

As they traveled, Hannah strained her neck in every direction to see if she could catch sight of the men and their caravan, but she did not see them anywhere. The wine merchant was not very happy about the tag-along and did nothing to hide his feelings. Hannah didn't know what to do. She was torn between the excitement of going home and the anxiety of wanting to warn the Magi. Then she remembered what her mother had told her before she left home. "When you do not know the path to travel, pray to God, and he will direct you."

Hannah closed her eyes and whispered a prayer. Abar turned his head and looked at her. In a voice dripping with mockery he laughed. "What are you doing? Praying to your God? Haven't you Jews figured out yet that he doesn't listen? I've given you a ride far enough. Get off my wagon!"

Abar barely stopped the wagon to allow Hannah to jump from the seat. He threw her small bundle at her and laughed as his wagon rumbled away.

Hannah stood in the middle of the crowded dusty road, stunned. People walked around her as if she weren't even there. She allowed herself to be pushed along with the crowd, unsure of what else she should do.

She walked for a long time, and evening began to settle around her. Her legs were tired and the small lunch Ursula had given her was long gone. Hannah felt so lost and confused. Rubbing the tired from her eyes she gazed up into the dark sky, one star caught her attention. She looked at it for a long time watching it sparkle and twinkle. Then she remembered! The Magi were following a star! This one was so bright, it must be the one! The star was in front of her, she was on the right road, and they must be ahead of her! All the weariness left and her spirits rose. She knew her prayer had been answered. People along the road were bedding down for the night. It had been a very long day but Hannah knew she must find the wise men; she began to run.

She ran as long as she could but the pain in her side finally made her stop. It was dark now and most of the lanterns had been put out. Hannah walked down the middle of the road, feeling it was safer, and the strange star lit her way. She could still smell the rich aromas of dinners that had been eaten earlier and her stomach growled. The smell of bread reminded her of the sweetbread her mother used to make and of how her family would all sit together at meal time, laughing and talking. Tears started running down her face as she remembered, so she started running again.

Through the night she would run as far as she could then walk, always moving forward. The sun was beginning to push away the darkness and people were putting out the last of the fires and gathering up their belongings. Everyone was on the move again.

Hannah hadn't seen any sign of the Magi. Unable to go any further she crumbled to the ground. It wasn't just the pains in her side from running that made her stop but also the pains of hunger and thirst. She was too miserable to even cry. She curled up in a defeated ball beside the road and fell fast asleep.

The sound of a grumbling camel woke her. Her head hurt and she was so thirsty. The road was now full of people and carts and the sun was high in the sky. Startled she realized she had slept too long. How would she catch up to the Magi now?

Hannah stood up slowly, forcing her legs to work. Unsure of what to do now she looked around her. Maybe she could beg for some food and ask someone for directions to her home, maybe even a ride. But then she remembered the baby and the hateful words of Herod. She had to give her warning. She heard the camel again and looked toward the noise. Squinting in the bright sun she saw a caravan of many people and camels. Her heart lifted. This must be them! With the last of her strength she began to run. As she got closer she started searching faces. Then she saw them. She tried to call out but her throat was so dry nothing came out. She tried to run faster but instead she tripped and down she fell. Her hunger and exhaustion had finally caught up to her and she blacked out.

Hannah stirred as someone put a cool cloth on her forehead. For a brief moment she thought she was home, but when she opened her eyes a stranger looked back at her. First she was afraid, but the look of concern on his face comforted her and she knew she was safe. It was Melchior one of the Magi and his voice sounded like the booming voice of a drum. She smiled to herself because she could tell he was trying to whisper, and not succeeding.

"Balthasar, she is finally awake."

Balthasar came over and gently put a bowl of tea to her lips. The warm liquid had been sweetened with honey; it soothed her parched throat and warmed her empty belly.

"Don't drink it too fast little one." Balthasar's voice was low and gentle and as warm as the tea.

The edge of her hunger was gone but her head was still pounding. Hannah slowly looked around. She was in a small, colorful tent lying on a beautiful rug. Hannah did not know how long she had been asleep, but she knew it must have been a while because it was dark outside. Through the tent flap she saw the stars and remembered. Quickly sitting up she tried to speak, but began coughing instead. Balthasar gave her some more tea and the coughing fit subsided. Only able to whisper, she delivered her message. He leaned in to hear what she was trying to say. "Don't go back to the King, he will kill you and the baby," then she could say no more and fell asleep.

Hannah awoke from a very dark deep sleep. Balthasar sat in the corner reading. He turned when he heard her moving, and brought her more of the honeyed tea. After taking a sip she pleaded "Don't go back to Herod, it's dangerous."

He smiled and quietly said, "It's alright little one, we were already warned, but how did you know?"

The sweet tea had soothed her throat but still she could only whisper. "I saw you, I was hiding behind the curtains," She stopped and looked down realizing she had just admitted to spying on adults.

Smiling, Balthazar encouraged her, "Go on, you are safe here."

Carefully she began speak, "I saw you when you were talking about the baby king and how Herod told you to come back and tell him so he could worship him too. He was lying! When you left he flew into a rage and said when he found out where the baby was he was going to send his soldiers to kill him." Hannah swallowed hard; her throat was scratchy and now that she had delivered her message all her courage and strength were gone. She looked up into Balthazar's face, tears began to stream down her face, "Can I go home now?"

Balthazar hugged the small girl and hummed to her until she quieted down. "Yes, little one, we will find a way to return you to your home. Now worry no more."

Just then Caspar burst into the tent, a bowl of soup in one hand and bread in the other. Hannah almost laughed; He wore a huge bright colored squared hat with a tassel that danced on top as he moved, and a beard that was so big she almost couldn't see his mouth. The laughter seemed to clear the air and bring life back to her. The weariness and heavy feelings she had had since she was taken from her home were gone. Caspar handed her the broth and dark brown bread, it smelled so wonderful. She began to eat and only stopped when she realized the men were standing there watching her and smiling. Caspar handed her a fine napkin and she wiped her chin and then the last of her tears. Finally full and safe she asked the question that had been nagging at her. "Why is this baby so important, why is he called a king and why does Herod hate him so much?"

Balthasar sat down beside her and began to explain the prophecies that said there would be a great star shining in the west signaling the birth of a child born of a virgin in the city of David. "He will go forth and minister unto the people in power and great glory and the multitudes will gather together to hear him. He will go among the children of men and those who are sick and afflicted will be healed by the power of God. He will become a Savior to all. He is the Son of the Eternal Father."

The words seemed strangely familiar to Hannah, and, at the same time, comforting.

The next morning, camp was full of activity and commotion. Everyone was working at tearing down and getting ready to move on, and was too busy to pay much attention to Hannah, let alone to stop and talk to her. She stood at the tent door wondering where she should go when Balthasar came up beside her and said, "We have made arrangements to send you home safely."

Hannah had one more question she wanted to ask. "Balthasar, what are you going to do when you see the baby king?"

Balthasar smiled. "We will worship him and give him gifts."

"What kind of gifts?" asked Hannah.

"Come see, little one." Balthasar led her to one of the wagons. He pulled back the tarps and opened a large box. Inside were three small chests.

The first one contained a pearly blue bottle the color of foam on the sea. When he opened it, the aroma brought back memories of home. Often her family would walk by the Temple and she could smell the musky burning of the frankincense. She knew it was a very costly gift. The second contained a bottle made of onyx with small clear stones. It looked like the night sky full of twinkling stars. Balthasar unstopped it and put a little of the oil on her forehead. Hannah knew instantly it was myrrh. The ladies of the court perfumed themselves with it. They favored it not only for its sweet smell but for its expense. The third chest was beautifully encrusted in precious jewels. When it was opened Hannah gasped. It was full of gold coins. She looked up at Balthasar in amazement. "These are the most precious gifts in the land, but they are not as precious as the child we will find by following the star."

Just as he was closing the chest of gold, Hannah reached into her pocket and pulled out the small coin her father had given her. It wasn't much, but it was all she had. She felt it was important to send it with the other gifts. The coin was worn from her constant touch, but its worth was still great to her. It reminded her of home and the love that was waiting there for her.

"Wait, Balthasar, will you take this with you? It isn't much, but it is all I have, and I want to give a gift to the baby king."

Balthasar smiled and took the small coin. He laid it on top of the gold. "May the Lord watch over and bless you, little one. Now we must go."

Full of joy, Hannah went to get her things and join the group taking her home.

Balthasar turned to put the precious gifts away. Looking at the small coin Hannah had given him, he realized it was a mite; the smallest currency of the Jewish people. But even though its worth was so minimal, especially among the other gifts, he knew it was more priceless than all the gold that surrounded it. He would make sure it was on top and explain the precious story behind it to the mother

of the child King when they reached their destination.

Balthasar looked into the heavens. The sun would set soon. It was time to begin their journey again: following The Star.

36201062R00035

Made in the USA
Columbia, SC
23 November 2018